CHILDREN'S SINGING GAMES

CHILDREN'S SINGING GAMES

With the tunes to which they are sung

COLLECTED & EDITED
BY
ALICE B GOMME

PICTURED IN BLACK & WHITE
BY
WINIFRED SMITH

DAVID NUTT IN THE STRAND
LONDON

© 1993 PRYOR PUBLICATIONS

75 Dargate Road, Yorkletts, Whitstable
Kent CT5 3AE

Tel. & Fax: (0227) 274655

ISBN 0946014 16 7
A CIP RECORD FOR THIS BOOK IS AVAILABLE
FROM THE BRITISH LIBRARY.

Printed and bound by
Whitstable Litho Printers Ltd., Whitstable.

To

MY BOYS

IN MEMORY OF THE HAPPY DAYS

WHEN WE PLAYED TOGETHER

LADY ALICE BERTHA GOMME (1852 - 1938) was the wife of George Laurence Gomme, a great organiser and successively Secretary, Director and finally, from 1890 - 1894, President of the Folk-Lore Society. In retrospect, her contribution to folk-lore, and in particular the folk-lore of childhood, was as great as his. His approach tended towards the theoretical, whilst in her greatest work, the two-volume *The Traditional Games of England, Scotland and Ireland* (1894/1898), there was much field work, and much consultation, and the books cover some eight hundred games. The two volumes of singing games, with help from Cecil Sharp, are an attractive presentation of some of this research very suitably supported by the black and white illustration of Winifred Smith. Indeed, it would be difficult to find such a perfect combination of talents. Children loved the volumes and many are found with hand colouring by children themselves. Alice Gomme's original interest in children's games was aroused by a Shropshire nurse, who was nurse to children of a friend of hers, and had taught the singing games she knew to the children she was looking after. She retained this interest through her long life. She died in her eighty-sixth year. Her contribution to children's literature was of great use to Iona & Peter Opis, sixty years later, when they compiled *The Lore and Language of School Children* (1959), *Children's Games in Street and Playground* (1969) and *The Singing Game* (1985).

PETER STOCKHAM
(February 1993)

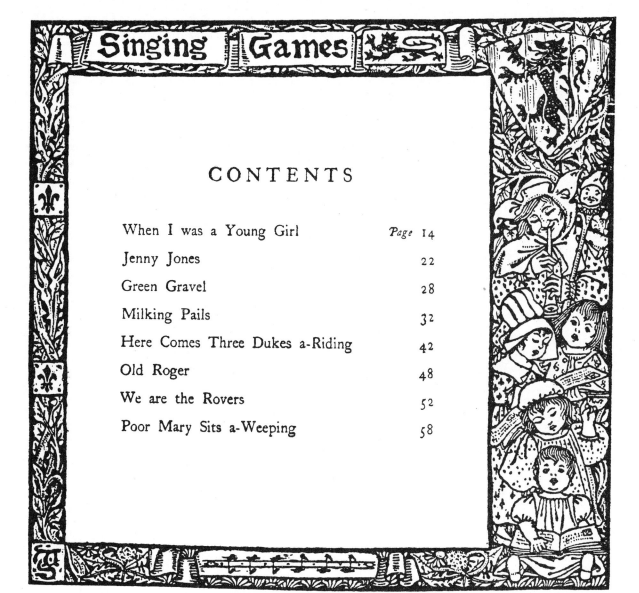

Singing Games

CONTENTS

WINIFRED SMITH did much of her illustrative work in the 1890's; she attended Birmingham School of Art, and was influenced by the Gaskins and other members of the Birmingham circle. She illustrated the two series of *Children's Singing Games*, the text being by Alice Gomme. In 1894 *The Bookman* described her as being an artist 'whose designs in black and white are witty, pretty and effective.'

In 1895, *Nursery Songs and Rhymes of England Pictured in Black and White* was published, probably her greatest achievement as an artist. In 1896 she won commendation in the National Competition at South Kensington, and *The Studio* magazine illustrated her work.

PETER STOCKHAM

PREFACE

A T a time when the amusement of children is more than ever considered to be an essential part of their up-bringing, it seems opportune to again introduce to those who do not know them otherwise, the traditional games preserved by generations of children. At almost every school where the delightful Kindergarten system is in vogue, the summer or winter concert generally includes one or more games. But good as these games are, they after all bear the stamp of their origin as one of the means for instruction. There is an absence of the wild unconsciousness of the traditional game and any one who watches, as I have done, such a game as, "Jenny Jones" played without the superintendence of any teacher or grown-up person, by the little children gambolling on the village greens out of school hours, or even in the murky and sunless courts of London, will at once recognise that there is a power in these games to fascinate and hold the minds of the players in a way that is almost unexplainable by description, and not to be obtained by the modern invented game. The pathos, the fun, and the "go" which

PREFACE

accompany every action of children while playing their own games, are unsurpassed and unsurpassable.

When one considers the conditions under which child-life exists in the courts of London (with which I am most acquainted), and of other great cities, it is almost impossible to estimate too highly the influence which these games have for good on town-bred populations. Of course, no mention is made of them in official statistics ; but I for one feel certain that no real criminal emanates from that large class of dirty, but withal healthy-looking, London children who play "When I was a Young Girl," and "Poor Mary sits a-Weeping," as if their very lives depended on the vigour and fervour they put into their movements. To those of my readers who are interested in London life or in the evolution of town life generally, I can promise considerable enjoyment by a visit to some of the slums and courts where these games are going on; and our reformers may learn a lesson from them, and perhaps see a way out of the dismal forebodings of what is to happen when the bulk of our population have deserted the country for the towns.

That it is possible to reduce the inequalities always perceptible on the village green, and still more so in the streets, and to arrive at good singing and good acting without losing one bit of the frolic and characteristic "go," was proved when in 1891 I presented, for the amusement of a

Singing Games

PREFACE

grown-up audience of Folkloreists from all parts of the world, some specimens of children's games from the village green of Barnes. For I am assured by the universal approbation which these items on the programme of the Conversazione at Mercers' Hall received, that these games, if faithfully reproduced from the traditional versions, are capable of giving great enjoyment to children who, alas! have not learnt them in the traditional method. It is one of the misfortunes of present-day society that our children lose the influences derived from the natural playing of games; but in every direction attention is being given in all classes to the necessities of recreation, and these games afford one of the most pleasant means of supplying that necessity.

There is one other aspect of these games which cannot but interest those who like to think and believe that their lives are linked indissolubly with the generations who have preceded us. Children are always mimics, or rather unconscious dramatists of the real events of life; and the action and words of some of these games are so divergent from present-day life, that we must look to the events of earlier periods for an explanation of them. It is impossible that they can have been invented by children by the mere effort of imagination, and there is ample evidence that they have but carried on unchangingly a record of events, some of which

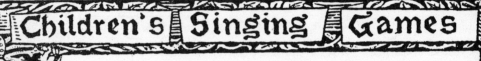
PREFACE

belong to the earliest days of the nation. In the Notes, I
have indicated where early customs appear to have been
enshrined in these games; and without devoting several
pages to prove these suggestions, I trust they may be
sufficiently evident to interest those of my readers who will
care more for the games when they know that they are
genuine records of the past, than if they were merely
presented as collections of the present day. This is not the
place to do more than state that children's games form a
section of folklore—those traditions, that is to say, which
are now being carefully studied as important contributions
to the past history of the nation.

This little book, then, goes forth to my little readers as a
message of happiness and fun from children who have
played the games it contains perhaps for centuries of time;
and it goes forth to those who will use it to teach the games
as a memorial of children's days, which few of us can
altogether afford to forget.

The tunes have been harmonised by my sister, Mrs.
F. Adam.

ALICE B. GOMME.

Barnes Common,
        March 1894.

12

WHEN·I·WAS·A·YOUNG·GIRL

When·I·had·a·sweetheart· Oh·this·way·went·I.

14

WHEN·I·WAS·A·YOUNG·GIRL

When I was a young girl a young girl a young girl when

I was a young girl how happy was I, and this way and that way and

this way and that way and this way and that way oh this way went I.

WHEN I WAS A YOUNG GIRL

When I was a schoolgirl, a schoolgirl, a schoolgirl.
When I was a schoolgirl, oh this way went I.
And this way and that way and this way and that way
When I was a schoolgirl, oh this way went I.

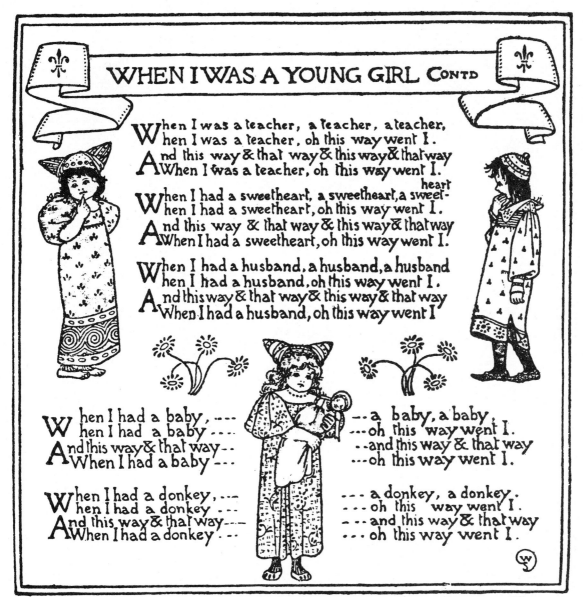

WHEN I WAS A YOUNG GIRL Contd

When I was a teacher, a teacher, a teacher,
When I was a teacher, oh this way went I.
And this way & that way & this way & that way
When I was a teacher, oh this way went I.

When I had a sweetheart, a sweetheart, a sweet-heart
When I had a sweetheart, oh this way went I.
And this way & that way & this way & that way
When I had a sweetheart, oh this way went I.

When I had a husband, a husband, a husband
When I had a husband, oh this way went I.
And this way & that way & this way & that way
When I had a husband, oh this way went I

When I had a baby, --- --- a baby, a baby,
When I had a baby --- --- oh this way went I.
And this way & that way -- --- and this way & that way
When I had a baby --- --- oh this way went I.

When I had a donkey, --- --- a donkey, a donkey.
When I had a donkey --- --- oh this way went I.
And this way & that way --- --- and this way & that way
When I had a donkey --- --- oh this way went I.

When I took in washing, oh washing, oh washing,
When I took in washing, oh this way went I.
And this way & that way & this way & that way
When I took in washing, oh this way went I.

When my baby died, oh died, oh died,
When my baby died, how sorry was I.
And this way & that way & this way & that way
When my baby died, oh this way went I.

When my husband died, oh died, oh died,
When my husband died, how sorry was I.
And this way & that way & this way & that way
When my husband died, oh this way went I.

DIRECTIONS FOR PLAYING

WHEN I WAS A YOUNG GIRL

Any Number of Children may Play

THE players join hands and form a ring. They all dance or walk round, finging the words and keeping the ring form until the end of the fecond line of each verfe. They then unclafp hands, ftand ftill, and (in the firft verfe) each child takes hold of her drefs with her hands and dances a ftep to the left and another to the right, two or three times, finging the other two lines of the verfe, and at the words "this way went I," turns herfelf right round in a pirouette, finifhing with her face to the centre of the ring. The children then all join hands again, and fing the two *firft* lines of the fecond verfe, then again ftop, unclafp their hands, walk round fingly, and fuit their actions to the words they have juft fung. This is continued throughout the game.

WHEN I WAS A YOUNG GIRL

The different actions are : *Dancing* for the first verse, as described above ; *Holding both hands together* to form a book for " school-girls," and walking slowly round as if learning lessons or reading ; *Hearing lessons*, and pretending to " rap hands with the cane " when acting Teacher ; *Kissing hands*, or " throwing a kiss " while walking round, for " when I had a sweetheart " ; *Walking round in couples*, arm-in-arm, for " when I had a husband " ; Pretending to *nurse and hush a baby* in the sixth verse ; Pretending to *drive a donkey*, by taking hold of each other's skirts and using an imaginary whip in the seventh ; Pretending to *wash and wring clothes* in the eighth ; *Putting handkerchiefs to their eyes* and pretending to cry in the ninth ; sitting on the ground, putting handkerchiefs or pinafores over the face and head, and rocking themselves backwards and forwards, as if in the deepest grief, for the last verse ; Always joining hands and walking round in a circle when singing the two first lines of each verse.

WE'VE·COME·TO·SEE·POOR·JENNY·JONES

Oh! Jenny is washing, washing, washing;
Oh! Jenny is washing
You can't see her now.

22

23

# JENNY JONES

MOTHER

Oh! Jenny is washing, washing, washing,
Oh! Jenny is washing, you can't see her now.

SUITORS

We've come to see poor Jenny Jones, Jenny Jones, Jenny Jones.
We've come to see poor Jenny Jones, how is she now?

MOTHER

Oh! Jenny is starching, starching, starching,
Oh! Jenny is starching, you can't see her now.

SUITORS

We've come to see poor Jenny Jones, Jenny Jones, Jenny Jones.
We've come to see poor Jenny Jones how is she now?

POOR·JENNY·JONES

Poor Jenny is dying

JENNY JONES CON^{TD}

MOTHER
Oh! Jenny is ironing, ironing, ironing,
Oh! Jenny is ironing, you can't see her now.

SUITORS
Jenny Jones
We've come to see poor Jenny Jones, Jenny Jones,
We've come to see poor Jenny Jones & how is she now?

MOTHER
Poor Jenny is ill, is ill, is ill,
Poor Jenny is ill, you can't see her now.

SUITORS
Jenny Jones
We've come to see poor Jenny Jones, Jenny Jones,
We've come to see poor Jenny Jones, & how is she now?

MOTHER
Poor Jenny is dying, is dying, is dying,
Poor Jenny is dying, you can't see her now.

SUITORS
Jenny Jones,
We've come to see poor Jenny Jones, Jenny Jones,
We've come to see poor Jenny Jones & how is she now?

MOTHER
Poor Jenny is dead, dead, dead,
Poor Jenny is dead. you can't see her now.

ALL
There's red for the Soldiers & blue for the sailors,
And black for the mourners of poor Jenny Jones.

Jenny Jones

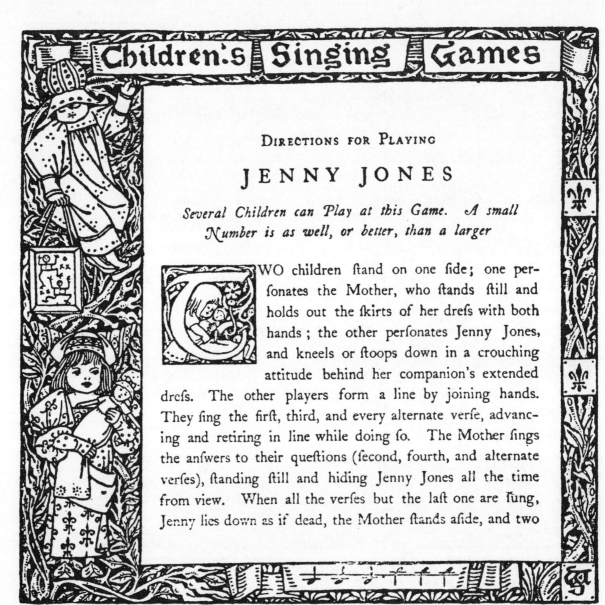

DIRECTIONS FOR PLAYING

JENNY JONES

Several Children can Play at this Game. A small Number is as well, or better, than a larger

TWO children stand on one side; one personates the Mother, who stands still and holds out the skirts of her dress with both hands; the other personates Jenny Jones, and kneels or stoops down in a crouching attitude behind her companion's extended dress. The other players form a line by joining hands. They sing the first, third, and every alternate verse, advancing and retiring in line while doing so. The Mother sings the answers to their questions (second, fourth, and alternate verses), standing still and hiding Jenny Jones all the time from view. When all the verses but the last one are sung, Jenny lies down as if dead, the Mother stands aside, and two

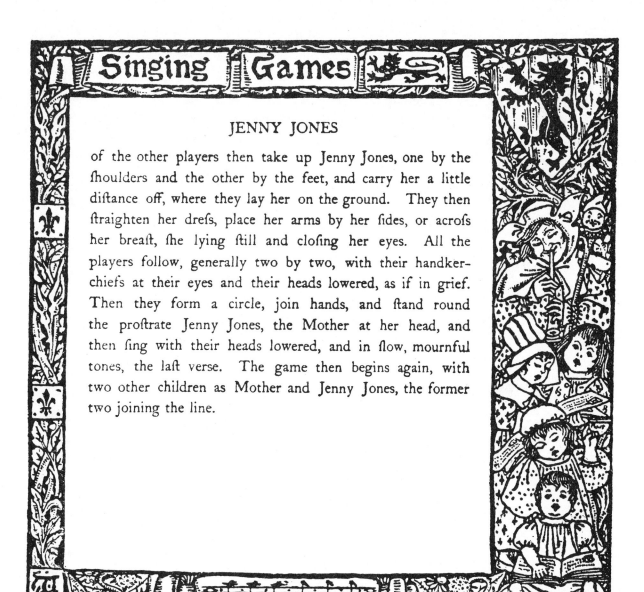

JENNY JONES

of the other players then take up Jenny Jones, one by the shoulders and the other by the feet, and carry her a little diftance off, where they lay her on the ground. They then ftraighten her drefs, place her arms by her fides, or acrofs her breaft, fhe lying ftill and clofing her eyes. All the players follow, generally two by two, with their handker-chiefs at their eyes and their heads lowered, as if in grief. Then they form a circle, join hands, and ftand round the proftrate Jenny Jones, the Mother at her head, and then fing with their heads lowered, and in flow, mournful tones, the laft verse. The game then begins again, with two other children as Mother and Jenny Jones, the former two joining the line.

27

28

GREEN GRAVEL

Green gravel, green gravel,
your grass is so green.

DIRECTIONS FOR PLAYING

GREEN GRAVEL

Any Number of Children may Play

THE children join hands and form a ring. They all walk round, keeping the ring form, and sing the words. When singing the fifth line, one of the children is "named" by the others, and at the end of the sixth line this child "turns her head" by turning round and *facing* the *outside* of the circle or ring, and having her *back* to the *inside*. She joins hands again with the other players, and the ring walks round singing the words again, another child being named and turning her face to the *outside* of the circle. This is continued until all the children face *outwards*, holding hands and walking round. In some places the game ends here; in others, it is continued until all the players have again reversed their positions and face the inside of the ring or circle, as at first.

Buy me a pair of new milk-
-ing pails   Gentle
sweet mother o' mine.

MILKING PAILS

Mary's gone a milking mother mother.

Mary's gone a milking Gentle sweet mother o' mine.

33

MILKING PAILS

Take your pails and go after her
        daughter, daughter.
Take your pails and go after her
Gentle sweet daughter o' mine.

Buy me a pair of new milking pails
        mother, mother.
Buy me a pair of new milking pails
Gentle sweet mother o' mine.

Where's the money to come from
        daughter, daughter.
Where's the money to come from
Gentle sweet daughter o' mine.

MILKING PAILS Contd

Mother

Daughter

Sell my father's feather bed
mother, mother.
Sell my father's feather bed
Gentle sweet mother o'mine.

What's your father to sleep in
daughter, daughter.
What's your father to sleep in
Gentle sweet daughter o'mine.

Put him in the children's bed
mother, mother.
Put him in the children's bed
Gentle sweet mother o'mine.

35

MILKING PAILS

Where shall the children go to [sleep]
daughter, daughter.
Where shall the children go to [sleep]
Gentle sweet daughter o'mine.

Put them in the pig stye
mother, mother.
Put them in the pig stye
Gentle sweet mother o'mine.

What shall the pigs lay in
daughter, daughter.
What shall the pigs lay in
Gentle sweet daughter o'mine.

Put them in the washing tub
mother, mother
Put them in the washing tub
Gentle sweet mother o'mine.

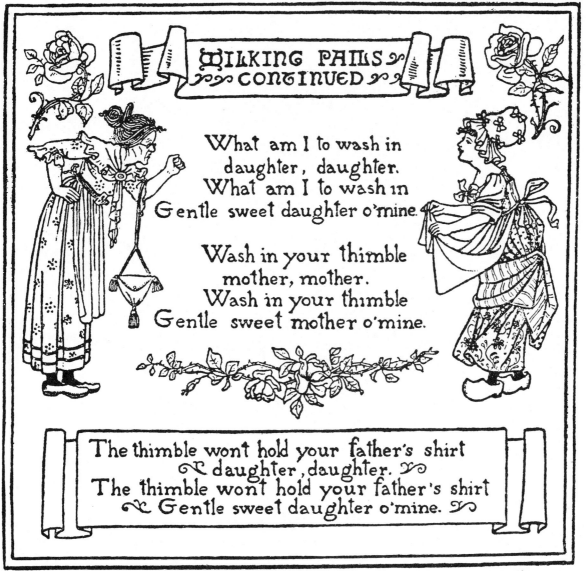

MILKING PAILS CONTINUED

What am I to wash in
daughter, daughter.
What am I to wash in
Gentle sweet daughter o'mine.

Wash in your thimble
mother, mother.
Wash in your thimble
Gentle sweet mother o'mine.

The thimble won't hold your father's shirt
daughter, daughter.
The thimble won't hold your father's shirt
Gentle sweet daughter o'mine.

Wash in the river
mother, mother.
Wash in the river

CONTINUED

MILKING PAILS

Gentle sweet
mother ৶৶
o' mine.

Suppose the clothes should blow away
daughter, daughter.
Suppose the clothes should blow away
Gentle sweet daughter o' mine.

W.S

WASH IN THE RIVER MOTHER

MILKING PAILS CONCLUDED

Set a man to watch them
   mother, mother.
Set a man to watch them
Gentle sweet mother o'mine.

Suppose the man should go to sleep
   daughter, daughter.
Suppose the man should go to sleep
Gentle sweet daughter o'mine.

Take a boat and go after them
   mother, mother.
Take a boat and go after them
Gentle sweet mother o'mine.

Suppose the boat should be upset
   daughter, daughter.
Suppose the boat should be upset
Gentle sweet daughter o'mine.

Then there would be an end of you
   mother, mother.
Then there would be an end of you
Gentle sweet mother o'mine.

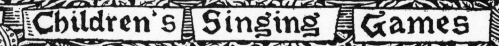

DIRECTIONS FOR PLAYING

MILKING PAILS

Any Number of Children may Play

ONE child stands apart from the rest and personates the Mother. She usually carries a stick. The other children form a line, holding hands and facing the Mother. They advance and retire, singing the first and every alternate verse, while the Mother stands still; then the Mother, advancing and retiring, in response sings the second and alternate verses, while the line stands still. While the last verse is being sung, the line of children all run off in different directions; the Mother runs after them, catches and beats them. The first or last one caught usually becomes Mother in the next set, the game continuing until all have personated the Mother.

Here come three Dukes a

ri‑ding a ri‑ding a

ri‑ding here come three Dukes a ri‑ding with a rancy tancy tay.

THREE · DUKES ·
✿✿✿ A · RIDING ·

What is your good will Sirs,
Will Sirs, will Sirs,
What is your good will Sirs?
With a rancy tancy tay!

Our good will is to marry,
To marry, to marry,
Our good will is to marry
With a rancy tancy tay!

Marry one of us Sirs,
Us Sirs, us Sirs,
Marry one of us Sirs
With a rancy tancy tay!

You're all too black & dirty
Dirty, dirty,
You're all too black & dirty
With a rancy tancy tay!

THREE DUKES CONTD

Last verse only

Thro' the kitchen & thro' the hall I choose the fairest of you all, the

fair-est one that I can see is pretty Miss———— walk with me.

We're good enough for you Sirs
You Sirs, you Sirs,
We're good enough for you Sirs,
With a rancy tancy tay!

You're all as stiff as pokers,
Pokers, pokers,
You're all as stiff as pokers
With a rancy tancy tay!

We can bend as well as you Sirs
You Sirs, you Sirs,
We can bend as well as you Sirs
With a rancy tancy tay!

HERE · COME · THREE · DUKES · A · RIDING

MARKETBOROUGH

Marry · one · of · us · Sirs ·
Us · Sirs · Us · Sirs ·
Marry · one · of · us · Sirs
With · a · rancy · tancy · tay ·

44

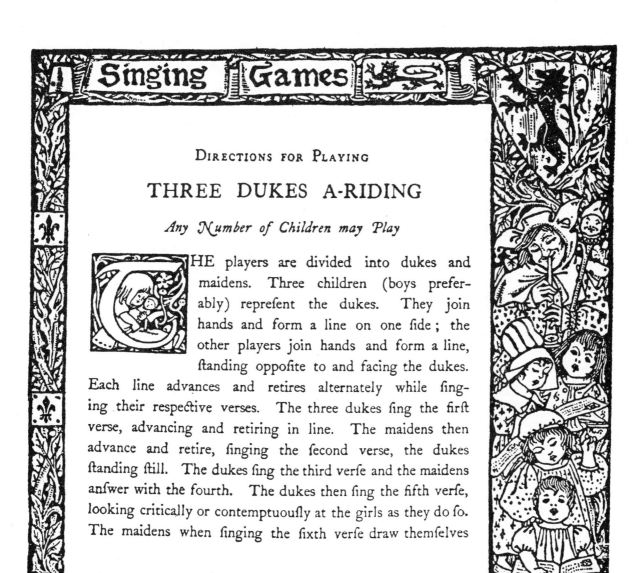

DIRECTIONS FOR PLAYING

THREE DUKES A-RIDING

Any Number of Children may Play

THE players are divided into dukes and maidens. Three children (boys preferably) reprefent the dukes. They join hands and form a line on one fide; the other players join hands and form a line, ftanding oppofite to and facing the dukes. Each line advances and retires alternately while finging their respective verses. The three dukes fing the firft verse, advancing and retiring in line. The maidens then advance and retire, finging the fecond verse, the dukes ftanding ftill. The dukes fing the third verfe and the maidens anfwer with the fourth. The dukes then fing the fifth verfe, looking critically or contemptuoufly at the girls as they do fo. The maidens when finging the fixth verfe draw themfelves

THREE DUKES A-RIDING

up, hold their heads as proudly as they can, and look offended. The dukes retort in the same manner as before, when singing the seventh verse. At the word "bend," in the eighth verse, the maidens all *bow* down their heads and bend their bodies as gracefully as they can, holding themselves erect afterwards. The dukes when singing the last verse, name the girl whom they choose. At the end of this verse, the girl named walks over to them and joins the line of dukes. The game is continued by the dukes singing the first verse again, saying : "Here come *four* dukes a-riding." The verses are sung over and over again, until all the maidens are ranged on the dukes' side, they adding one to their number every time.

· OLD · ROGER · · ·

They planted an apple tree over his head
H'm! ha!   over his head

The apples were ripe and ready to drop
H'm! ha!   ready to drop.

There came an old woman a picking them up
H'm! ha!   picking them up.

Old Roger jumped up and gave her a knock
H'm! ha!   gave her a knock .

Which made that old woman go hippity hop
H'm! ha!   hippity hop.

W·S

48

OLD ROGER

Old Ro--ger is dead and gone to his grave

H'm! ha! gone to his grave.

DIRECTIONS FOR PLAYING

OLD ROGER

Any Number of Children can Play this Game

ONE child, who reprefents Old Roger, lies down on the ground, either having his face and head covered with a handkerchief, or a cloak or apron is thrown all over him, completely covering his body. Two other children ftand apart, and the reft of the players ftand round the dead Old Roger in a circle, and only they fing the words. Thefe children ftand ftill throughout the game, croffing their arms over their breafts, bending their heads and fwaying their bodies backwards and forwards in a mourning attitude, while they fing the firft verfe. At the commencement of the fecond verfe, one of the two children who are ftanding apart goes into the circle and ftands befide Old Roger's head, to reprefent the apple tree.

OLD ROGER

During the finging of the third verfe, this child raifes his arms above his fhoulders and drops them again, to fhow the falling apples. At the commencement of the fourth verfe, the other outfide child goes into the circle to reprefent the old woman, and pretends to pick up the fallen fruit. Then, at the beginning of the next verfe, Old Roger jumps up and beats the Old Woman out of the ring, who goes off during the finging of the laft verfe, hobbling on one foot as if crippled and hurt. The game then begins again, with three other children as the actors, the previous three joining the circle. There is no interval between the verfes.

WE · ARE · THE · ROVERS

We are coming to take your land

We are coming to take your land   We are   the   Ro----vers

We are coming to take your land though you're the Guardian Sol---diers

WE ARE THE ROVERS
CON- -TINUED

We don't care for your men nor [you]
    Though you're the Rovers
We don't care for your men nor [you]
For we're the Guardian Soldiers.

We will send our dogs to bite
    We are the Rovers
We will send our dogs to bite
Though you're the Guardian Soldiers.

We don't care for your dogs nor [you]
    Though you're the Rovers
We don't care for your dogs nor [you]
For we're the Guardian Soldiers.

Will you have a glass of wine
    We are the Rovers
Will you have a glass of wine
For respect of Guardian Soldiers.

WE ARE THE ROVERS

CONCLUDED

A glass of wine wont serve us all
    Though youre the Rovers,
A glass of wine wont serve us all
For we're the Guardian Soldiers.

A barrel of beer wont serve us all
    Though you're the Rovers,
A barrel of beer wont serve us all
For we're gallant Guardian Soldiers.

We dont fear your blue-coat men
    Though you're the Rovers,
We don't fear your blue-coat men
For we're the Guardian Soldiers.

We don't mind your red-coat men
    Though you're the Rovers,
We don't mind your red-coat men
For we're the Guardian Soldiers

Will a barrel of beer then serve | you all
    We are the Rovers, | you all
Will a barrel of beer then serve
As you're the Guardian Soldiers.

We will send our blue coat men
    We are the Rovers,
We will send our blue coat men
Though you're the Guardian Soldiers

We will send our red-coat men
    We are the Rovers,
We will send our red-coat men
    Though you're the Guardian Soldiers

Are you ready for a fight
    We are the Rovers,
Are you ready for a fight
Though you're the Guardian Soldiers

Yes! we're ready for a fight
    Though you're the Rovers
Yes! we're ready for a fight
For were the Guardian Soldiers
Present! Shoot! Bang! Fire.

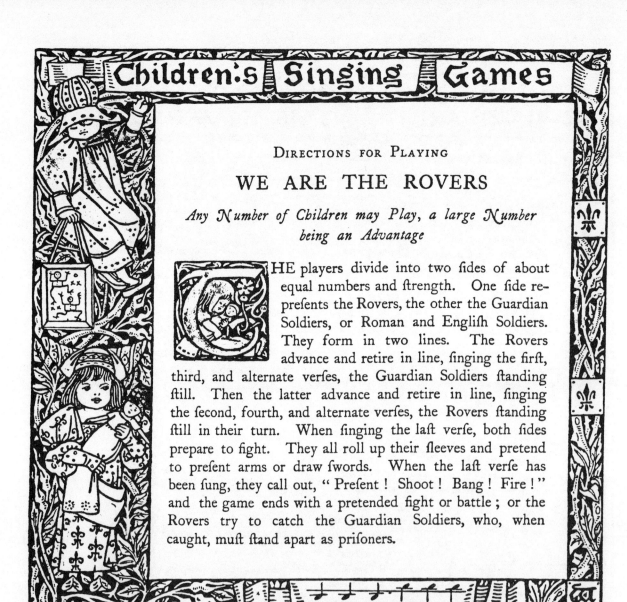

DIRECTIONS FOR PLAYING

WE ARE THE ROVERS

Any Number of Children may Play, a large Number being an Advantage

THE players divide into two sides of about equal numbers and strength. One side represents the Rovers, the other the Guardian Soldiers, or Roman and English Soldiers. They form in two lines. The Rovers advance and retire in line, singing the first, third, and alternate verses, the Guardian Soldiers standing still. Then the latter advance and retire in line, singing the second, fourth, and alternate verses, the Rovers standing still in their turn. When singing the last verse, both sides prepare to fight. They all roll up their sleeves and pretend to present arms or draw swords. When the last verse has been sung, they call out, " Present ! Shoot ! Bang ! Fire ! " and the game ends with a pretended fight or battle ; or the Rovers try to catch the Guardian Soldiers, who, when caught, must stand apart as prisoners.

POOR MARY SITS A WEEPING

THE COUNTRY GIRL

Pray Mary what are you weeping for? I'm weeping for a sweetheart Pray Mary choose your lover

POOR MARY SITS A WEEPING

Poor Ma-ry sits a weeping a weeping a weeping, Poor
Ma--ry sits a weeping on a bright summer's day.

Pray Mary what are you weeping for
A weeping for, a weeping for,
Pray Mary what are you weeping for
On a bright summers day.

I'm weeping for a sweetheart
A sweetheart, a sweetheart
I'm weeping for a sweetheart
On a bright summers day

Pray Mary choose your lover
Your lover, your lover,
Pray Mary choose your lover
On a bright summers day.

DIRECTIONS FOR PLAYING

POOR MARY SITS A WEEPING

Any Number of Children can Play

A RING is formed by all the players except one joining hands. The odd player kneels down on the ground in the centre of the ring, covering her face with her hands. The ring of children dance round her singing the firſt two verses. The kneeling child then takes her hands from her face and sings the third verſe alone, ſtill kneeling, while the ring dances round. The ring of children then ſing the fourth verſe, ſtill dancing round. While they are ſinging this, the kneeling child riſes and chooſes any child she pleaſes from the ring, who goes into the centre with her. These two both ſtand or dance round together, holding hands while the ring ſing the marriage formula, and they kiſs each other at the command. The ring dances round much more quickly during the ſinging of this laſt verſe. The child who was "Poor Mary" then joins the ring and the child who had been choſen by her kneels down, and the game begins again.

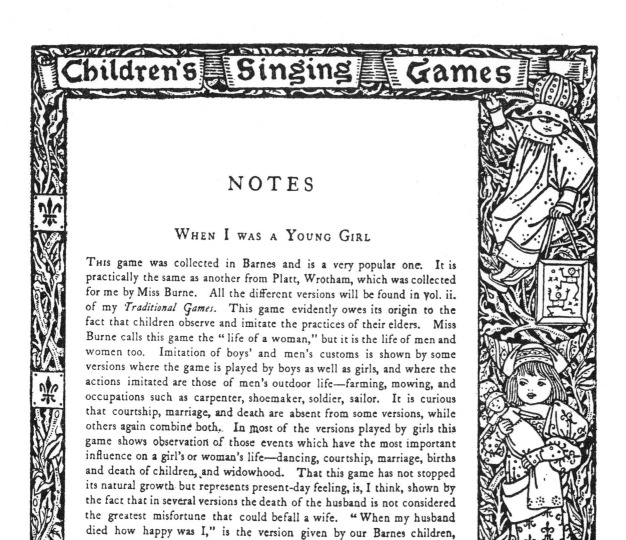

NOTES

WHEN I WAS A YOUNG GIRL

THIS game was collected in Barnes and is a very popular one. It is practically the same as another from Platt, Wrotham, which was collected for me by Miss Burne. All the different versions will be found in vol. ii. of my *Traditional Games*. This game evidently owes its origin to the fact that children observe and imitate the practices of their elders. Miss Burne calls this game the "life of a woman," but it is the life of men and women too. Imitation of boys' and men's customs is shown by some versions where the game is played by boys as well as girls, and where the actions imitated are those of men's outdoor life—farming, mowing, and occupations such as carpenter, shoemaker, soldier, sailor. It is curious that courtship, marriage, and death are absent from some versions, while others again combine both. In most of the versions played by girls this game shows observation of those events which have the most important influence on a girl's or woman's life—dancing, courtship, marriage, births and death of children, and widowhood. That this game has not stopped its natural growth but represents present-day feeling, is, I think, shown by the fact that in several versions the death of the husband is not considered the greatest misfortune that could befall a wife. "When my husband died how happy was I," is the version given by our Barnes children, (it is thought advisable in this book to give the orthodox termination);

NOTES

to this waving of handkerchiefs as a signal of rejoicing and a final "Hurrah ! !" ends the game. Many women grieve more for the loss of a baby than the loss of a husband ; the woman has, during her husband's lifetime, in so many cases to provide for herself and children, the man's money (when a small amount only is earned) is spent principally on himself ; the death of the husband in cases of drunkenness, too, considerably simplifies matters.

Now, too, that boys' and girls' schools are in separate buildings the playing together of boys and girls is practically at an end, and the boys' part of this game is dying out, while the girls alter their employments or occupations to suit their surroundings, learning lessons and teaching taking the place of more domestic employments.

Jenny Jones

This version was collected by Miss Burne from Platt, Wrotham, and was one of the games given at the Folklore Congress Conversazione. Many different versions are given in my *Traditional Games*, vol. i. pp. 260–277, as well as a detailed account of the methods of playing in different places, and the relative importance of these. The game as presented in this version, and as generally played, shows only a dramatic rendering of a funeral of earlier times, but there is evidence in some of the versions to show that the game was formerly one of courting, ending in the death and burial of one of the lovers, and I suggest its origin from the early village custom of a band of suitors wooing the girls of a village. Many

NOTES

versions show that the colour selected is the one to dress the corpse in. The dressing of the corpse of a maiden in white, and the carrying it to the grave by girl companions, is a well-known village custom, and was practised in some parts until a not very recent period. In some versions, too, an important incident, that of "ghost," or spirit of the dead, occurs. The dead Jenny, after the burial is accomplished, springs up and pursues the mourners, who scatter in all directions, calling out, "The ghost! the ghost!" This rising of the dead lover is another illustration of the old belief that spirits of the unquiet dead rise from their graves, haunt churchyards and places of their former abodes.

GREEN GRAVEL

THIS game was collected (words and tune) from Barnes children. This game, the version of which given in this book is the one most prevalent, is described in my *Traditional Games*, vol. i. pp. 170–183, rather fully, and an analysis of the incidents from all variants is also given, the result of which shows the game to have been originally connected with funeral ceremonies. Green Gravel is probably "green grave," and the incidents of washing and dressing the corpse and writing an inscription, important functions as these were in earlier times, are all indicated, as well as the belief of communion with the dead. In many versions, love and marriage verses occur. These may or may not be later interpolations. An old funeral ceremony, known as "Dish-a-loof," illustrates the action of the players in "turning back their heads." During this ceremony the

H

NOTES

watchers at a funeral went out of the room (where the corpse was lying) and returned into it backwards.

In Shropshire (Madeley) this game of "Green Gravel" is always played with the game of "Wallflowers," as one game. This indicates the death of the players while maidens, consequently unmarried or betrothed girls. Miss Burne considers these two games were meant to go together. They may be part of one original game.

MILKING PAILS

THIS version, both words and tune, was told me by a London nursemaid. It is almost identical with some variants collected for me in different parts of the country during the last two or three years, although many of these later collected versions show that the game is in a decaying stage. "Milk-pails," which were formerly pails of wood suspended from a yoke, carried on the milkmaid's shoulders, have in some versions become "milking cans" to suit present-day requirements. See versions from South Shields, Swaffham, and Cowes, given in my *Traditional Games*, pp. 385, 386. References are also given to the former use of the old box and truckle beds which are mentioned in the game. The origin of this game is probably to be attributed to purely country life, to the time when the possession of one or two beds was considered sufficient for the family; when outdoor washing and bleaching home-spun linen by the rivers and streams were in vogue, and when the summer shealings for cheese and butter annually took place.

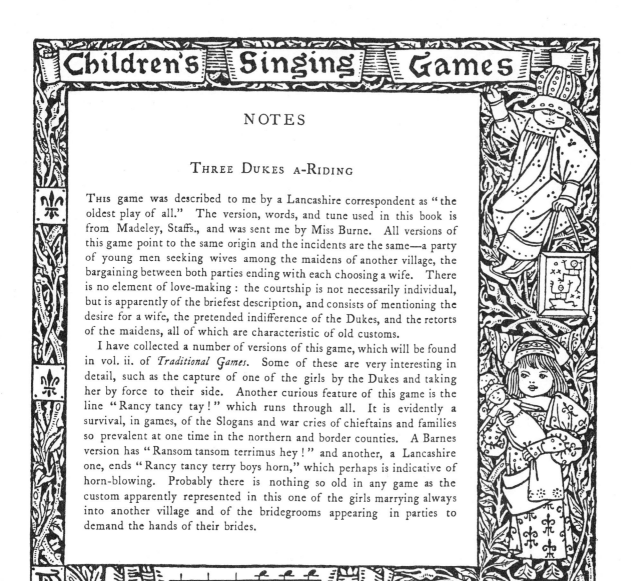

NOTES

THREE DUKES A-RIDING

THIS game was described to me by a Lancashire correspondent as "the oldest play of all." The version, words, and tune used in this book is from Madeley, Staffs., and was sent me by Miss Burne. All versions of this game point to the same origin and the incidents are the same—a party of young men seeking wives among the maidens of another village, the bargaining between both parties ending with each choosing a wife. There is no element of love-making : the courtship is not necessarily individual, but is apparently of the briefest description, and consists of mentioning the desire for a wife, the pretended indifference of the Dukes, and the retorts of the maidens, all of which are characteristic of old customs.

I have collected a number of versions of this game, which will be found in vol. ii. of *Traditional Games*. Some of these are very interesting in detail, such as the capture of one of the girls by the Dukes and taking her by force to their side. Another curious feature of this game is the line "Rancy tancy tay !" which runs through all. It is evidently a survival, in games, of the Slogans and war cries of chieftains and families so prevalent at one time in the northern and border counties. A Barnes version has "Ransom tansom terrimus hey !" and another, a Lancashire one, ends "Rancy tancy terry boys horn," which perhaps is indicative of horn-blowing. Probably there is nothing so old in any game as the custom apparently represented in this one of the girls marrying always into another village and of the bridegrooms appearing in parties to demand the hands of their brides.

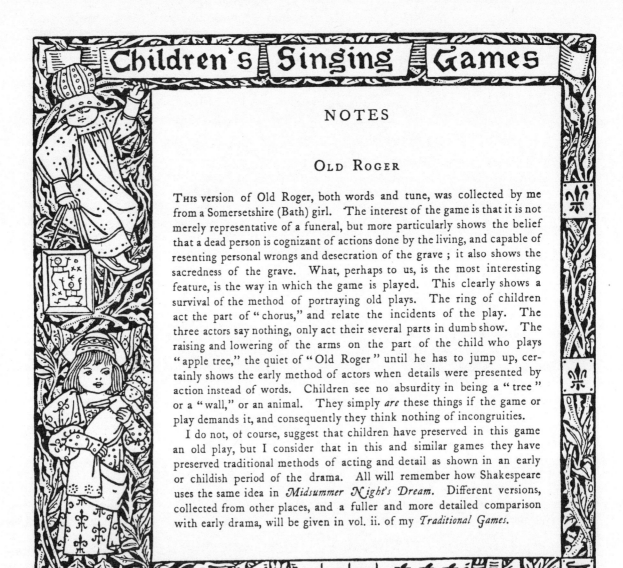

NOTES

OLD ROGER

THIS version of Old Roger, both words and tune, was collected by me from a Somersetshire (Bath) girl. The interest of the game is that it is not merely representative of a funeral, but more particularly shows the belief that a dead person is cognizant of actions done by the living, and capable of resenting personal wrongs and desecration of the grave ; it also shows the sacredness of the grave. What, perhaps to us, is the most interesting feature, is the way in which the game is played. This clearly shows a survival of the method of portraying old plays. The ring of children act the part of "chorus," and relate the incidents of the play. The three actors say nothing, only act their several parts in dumb show. The raising and lowering of the arms on the part of the child who plays "apple tree," the quiet of "Old Roger" until he has to jump up, certainly shows the early method of actors when details were presented by action instead of words. Children see no absurdity in being a "tree" or a "wall," or an animal. They simply *are* these things if the game or play demands it, and consequently they think nothing of incongruities.

I do not, of course, suggest that children have preserved in this game an old play, but I consider that in this and similar games they have preserved traditional methods of acting and detail as shown in an early or childish period of the drama. All will remember how Shakespeare uses the same idea in *Midsummer Night's Dream.* Different versions, collected from other places, and a fuller and more detailed comparison with early drama, will be given in vol. ii. of my *Traditional Games.*

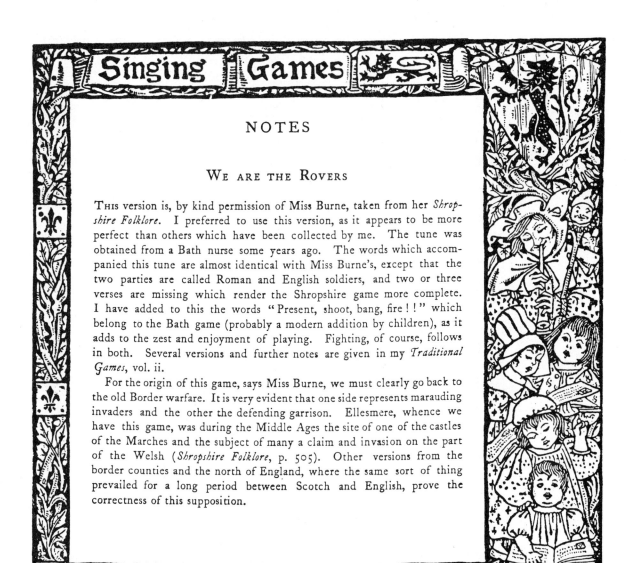

NOTES

WE ARE THE ROVERS

This version is, by kind permission of Miss Burne, taken from her *Shropshire Folklore*. I preferred to use this version, as it appears to be more perfect than others which have been collected by me. The tune was obtained from a Bath nurse some years ago. The words which accompanied this tune are almost identical with Miss Burne's, except that the two parties are called Roman and English soldiers, and two or three verses are missing which render the Shropshire game more complete. I have added to this the words "Present, shoot, bang, fire!!" which belong to the Bath game (probably a modern addition by children), as it adds to the zest and enjoyment of playing. Fighting, of course, follows in both. Several versions and further notes are given in my *Traditional Games*, vol. ii.

For the origin of this game, says Miss Burne, we must clearly go back to the old Border warfare. It is very evident that one side represents marauding invaders and the other the defending garrison. Ellesmere, whence we have this game, was during the Middle Ages the site of one of the castles of the Marches and the subject of many a claim and invasion on the part of the Welsh (*Shropshire Folklore*, p. 505). Other versions from the border counties and the north of England, where the same sort of thing prevailed for a long period between Scotch and English, prove the correctness of this supposition.

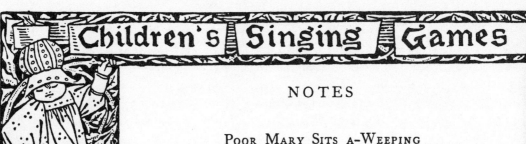

NOTES

Poor Mary Sits a-Weeping

THIS very popular kissing game was, both words and tune, collected by me in Barnes, and was one of those played at the Conversazione of the Folklore Congress in 1891. The game is descriptive of a marriage with the elements of love and courtship by individual choice. It contains also the usual marriage formula which is significant of the marriage being agreed to and ratified in the presence of witnesses (the ring of children) or by a priest. Then, too, must be noticed the line, " Seven years after, son and daughter," which probably refers to the old notion, which still lingers, I believe, in some places, of the marriage being terminable after that period. "A year and a day," and "seven years," are the two most popular notions of the period necessary for lovers and betrothed couples to remain faithful to each other. An important fact is that in these and other kiss-in-the-ring games, the tune of the marriage formula is always the same. The peculiar interest of a game like this lies in the fact that it may contain relics of the actual marriage ceremony of our earliest ancestors before it was made an institution of the Church. Different versions and illustrations of the game are given in *Traditional Games*, vol. ii.

———

These notes do not exhaust the evidence to prove that children's games contribute to the knowledge of our past social and domestic history, but they indicate, I hope, some of the interest which attaches to an investigation of even nursery antiquities.

DAVID NUTT IN THE STRAND

LOUD & CO.,
59 LONG ACRE, W.C.

CHILDREN'S SINGING GAMES

SECOND SERIES

1894

DAVID NUTT IN THE STRAND

A SECOND SERIES OF CHILDREN'S SINGING GAMES WILL BE PUBLISHED
IN AUGUST 1993 IN THE SAME FORMAT AS THE SERIES IT CONTAINS.

London Bridge is Broken Down	Round and Round the Village
Sally Water	The Jolly Miller
Three Sailors	Oats and Beans and Barley
Looby Loo	Here we Come up the Green Grass

With more superb illustrations by Winifred Smith, this book is a further
celebration of the work of Alice Gomme.

Size 235mm x 226mm Landscape
74 Pages Hardback

ISBN 0946014 13 2

Price £7.⁹⁹

This facsimile of *"Nursery Songs and Rhymes of England Pictured in Black and White,"* first published in 1895, will have wide appeal. There are 25 nursery songs and rhymes in all, with superb illustrations by Winifred Smith, some of her finest work. This is a book that has long needed to be re-published, equally as part of our heritage as for the book's charm and simplicity.

Size 227mm x 250mm
66 Pages Hardback

ISBN 094 6014 14 0

Price **£7.99**

A full list of our publications sent free on request.